To Isla and Ruaridh with love ~ TK

For Theodore ~ EE

Bloomsbury Publishing, London, New Delhi, New York and Sydney

First published in Great Britain in 2015 by Bloomsbury Publishing Plc
50 Bedford Square, London, WC1B 3DP

A CIP catalogue record for this book is available from the British Library

ISBN 978 1 4088 4935 4 (HB)
ISBN 978 1 4088 4936 1 (PB)

Printed in China by Leo Paper Products, Heshan, Guangdong
1 3 5 7 9 10 8 6 4 2

www.bloomsbury.com

all aboard the
DINOSAUR
EXPRESS

Timothy Knapman   Ed Eaves

BLOOMSBURY
LONDON   NEW DELHI   NEW YORK   SYDNEY

We're crowding on the platform, waiting for our train.

We try to catch a glimpse of it: we stretch and squeeze and strain.

A young Triceratops is first to see the cloud of steam.
"The Dinosaur Express is coming!" everybody screams.

The engine's like a T-Rex head, the carriages have scales!

It's faster than a pterosaur – it **flies** along the rails!

The Stegosaurus Stationmaster blows his whistle – **YES!**

"All aboard! All aboard the Dinosaur Express!"

Like a pterodactyl's wings, the doors flap open wide.
"Whoopee!" we cry and eagerly we run to get inside.

The seats, like allosaurus paws, are comfy as can be –
I get one by the window: there's so much I want to see!

The Stationmaster waves a flag and calls out, "Mind the doors!"
We hear a mighty HISS! CHUG-CHUG! and then the engine roars!

We're off! And just like that, our great adventure has begun.

Our prehistoric world **zooms** by, shining in the sun.

A kind ankylosaurus stops her trolley by my seat.

"Are you having fun?" she asks. "What would you like to eat?

A sandwich or a sticky bun? Just ask me and it's yours –

these are for the plant-eaters, and those for carnivores."

And who's got room for monster cake? I think that you can guess.

Oh, everything tastes yummy on the **Dinosaur Express!**

"**Tickets please!**" the Guard calls out,
as he comes walking through.
"Now someone's got a special
ticket – maybe one of you!"

He takes mine, and he clips it . . . I feel wobbly! I feel cold!
I'm the lucky dinosaur! **Check out that flash of gold!**

The Guard and I walk through the train as all the others cheer.

But what treat have I got in store? **I've simply no idea!**

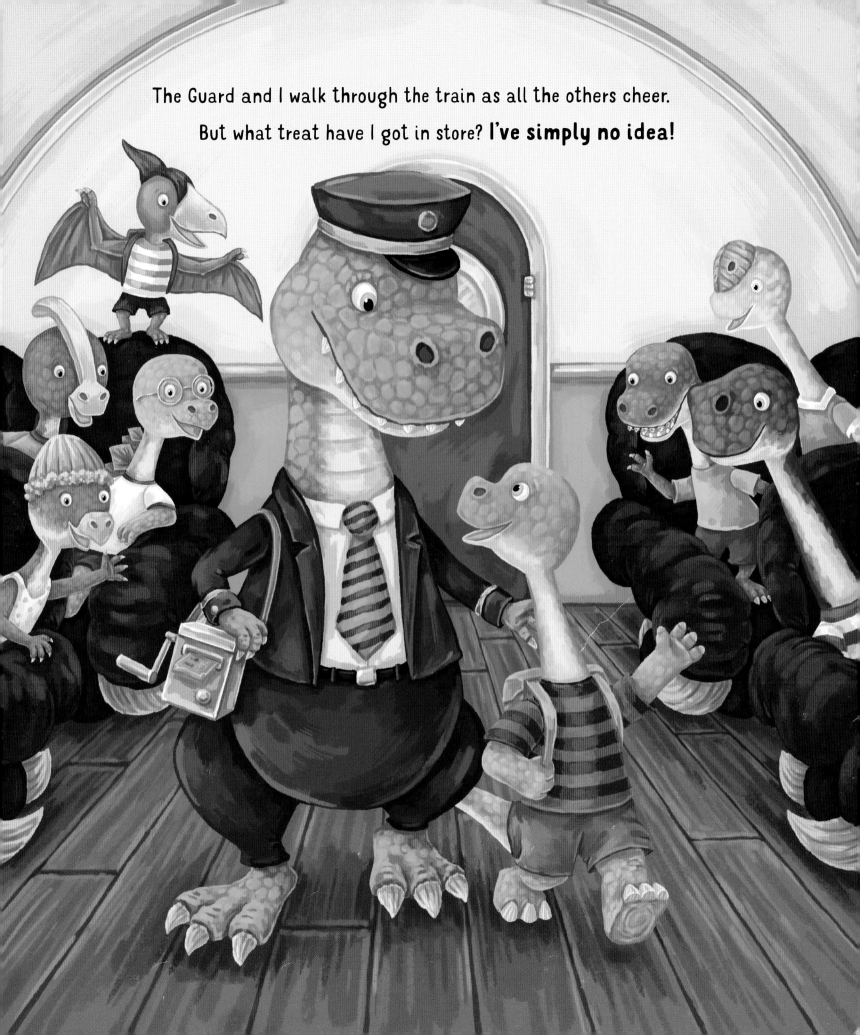

We reach the Driver's cabin and it's like a dream come true.

It's full of brontosaurus buttons! (What does that one do?)

The Driver says, **"Congratulations!** Now let me explain.

Your treat is this, young dinosaur: **you get to drive the train!"**

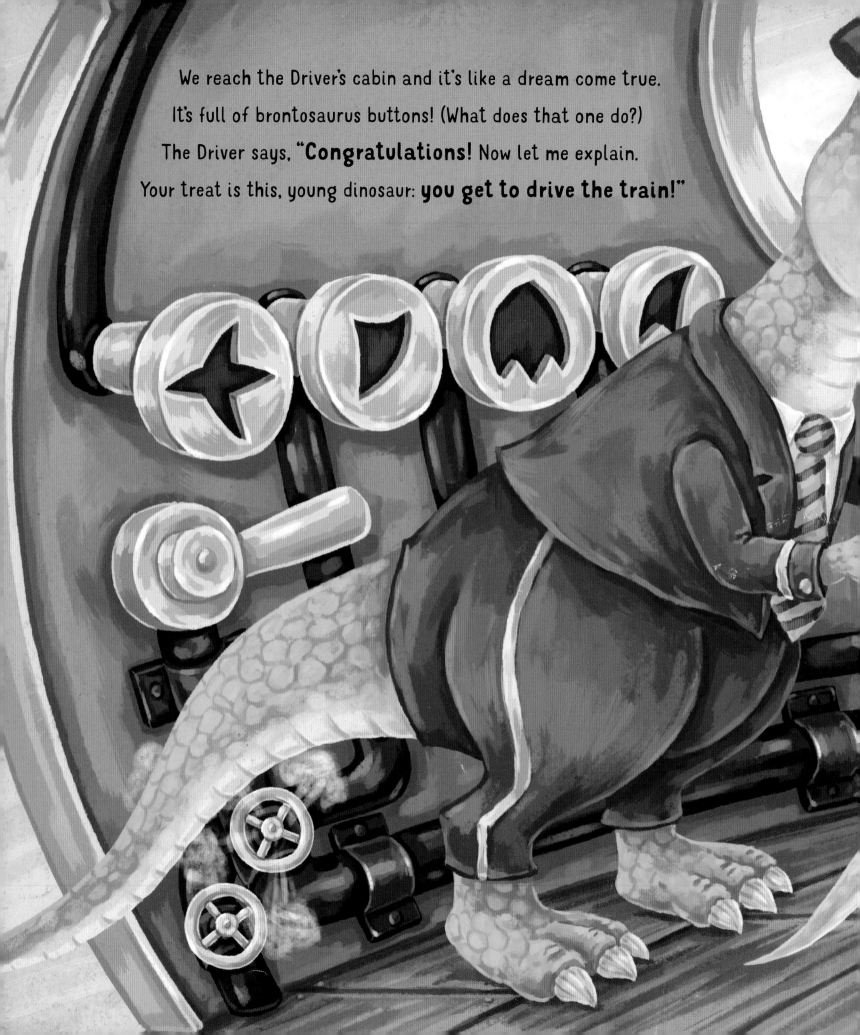

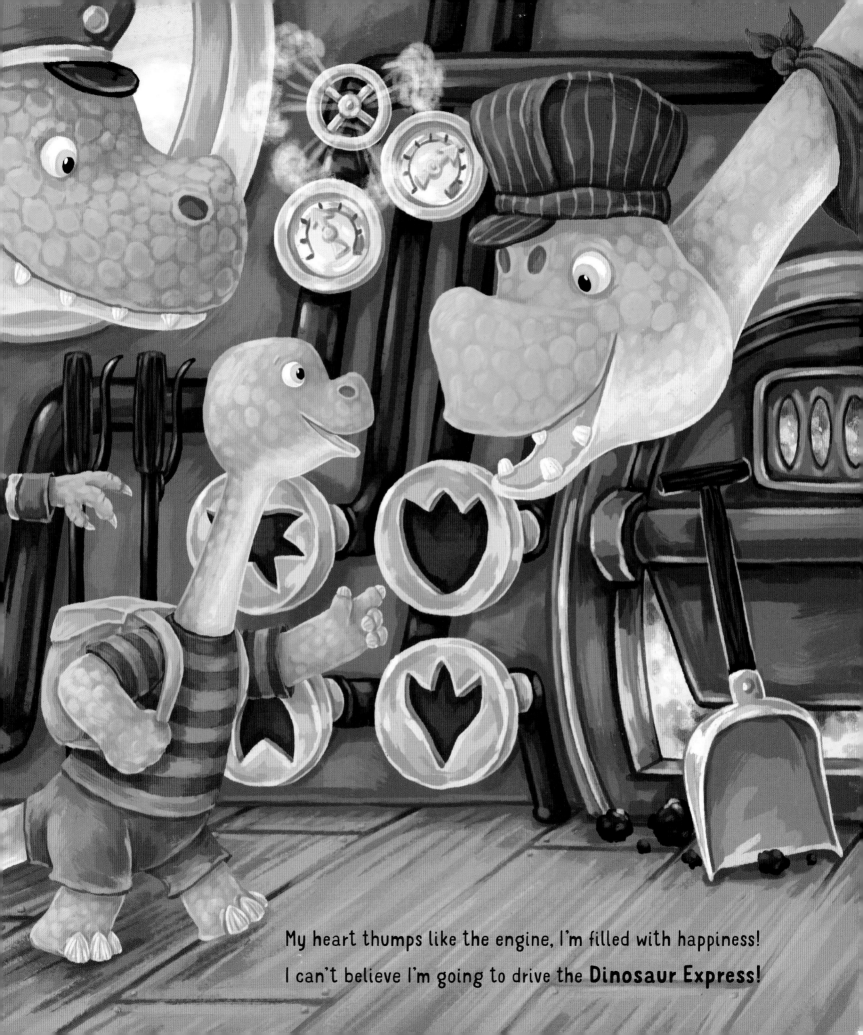

My heart thumps like the engine, I'm filled with happiness!
I can't believe I'm going to drive the **Dinosaur Express!**

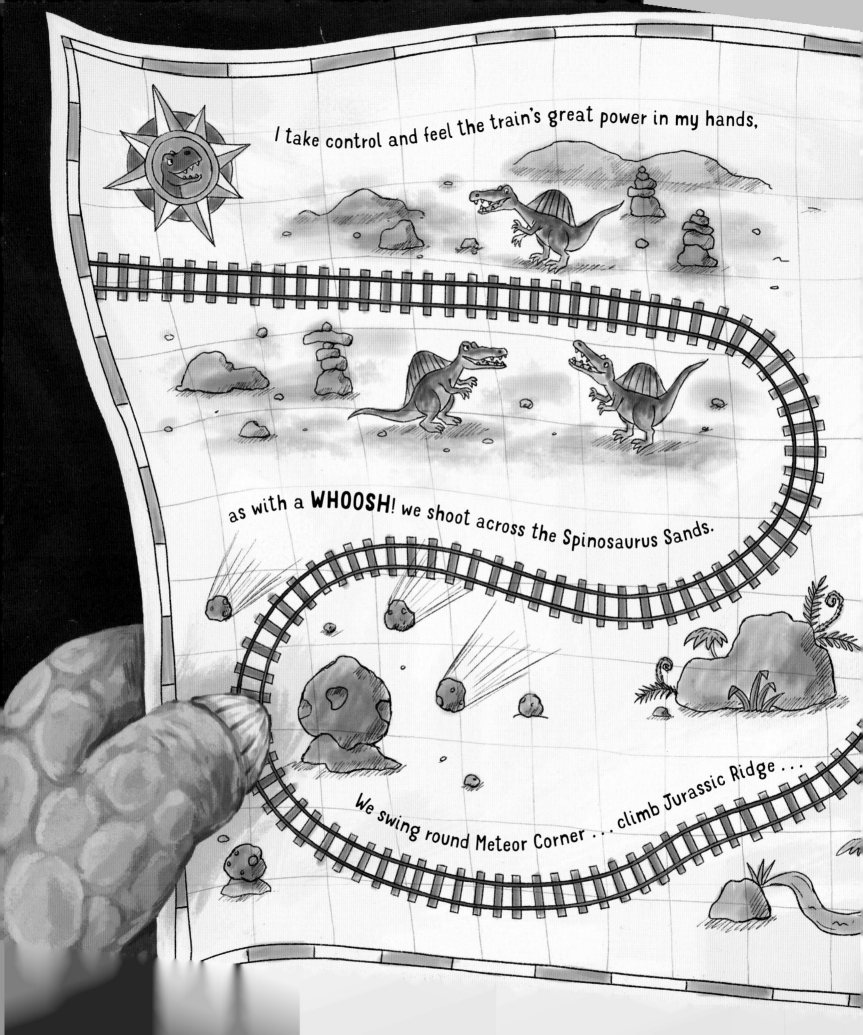

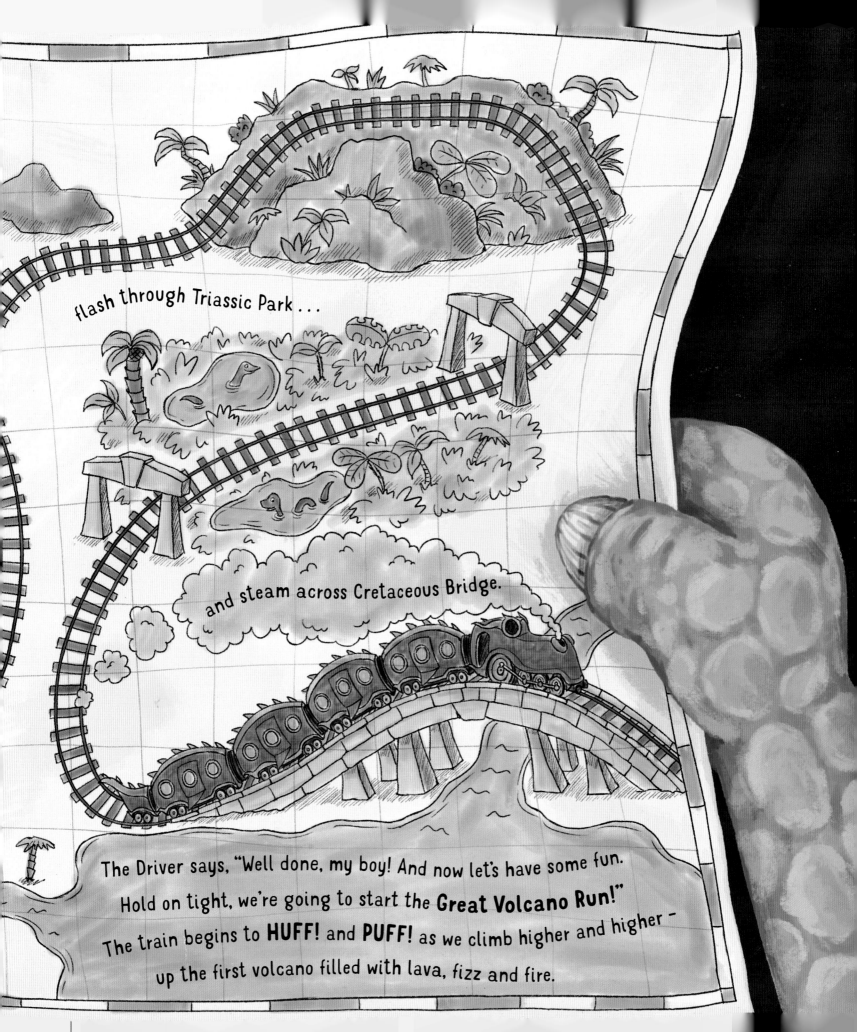

flash through Triassic Park . . .

and steam across Cretaceous Bridge.

The Driver says, "Well done, my boy! And now let's have some fun.
Hold on tight, we're going to start the **Great Volcano Run!**"
The train begins to **HUFF!** and **PUFF!** as we climb higher and higher –
up the first volcano filled with lava, fizz and fire.

We reach the top, I shout, "**Let's go!**" and down we roll like thunder.
We zigzag round three more volcanoes then – this is the wonder –
we **loop-the-loop**, and, **UPSIDE DOWN** we fly across the last.
We're steaming, roaring – dino-soaring – racing super-fast!

We safely reach the other side. I blow the whistle: **TWEET!**

And all too soon it's time for me to go back to my seat.

The Driver lets me keep his cap, the Guard gives me a flag;

with all these toys and souvenirs there's no room in my bag!

We chug back to the station – and there are Mum and Dad!

I tell them both about the wild adventure I've just had.

"I drove that mighty engine that looks like a T-Rex head!"

And I don't finish telling them until it's time for bed.

I go to sleep and dream about the job I want to do
when I'm a grown-up dinosaur (you'll want to do it too!).

I know that if I get a chance, I'll be a great success:
I'm going to be the driver of the **Dinosaur Express!**